Alice, An Alaska Pioneer tells the story of an imaginative six-year-old girl who leaves the comforts of her grandmother's Pennsylvania home at the end of World War II and learns to love life in a small, rural Alaska community.

Alice, an Alaska Pioneer
A Novel

Sara Budinger Peterson

Many of the events in this story actually happened in Homer, Alaska, in the years after World War II. The characters in the story are fictional, but some are based on people who lived in Homer at this time and were too interesting to fabricate.

Published by Saranjon Publishing, 1998
Homer, Alaska 99603.

ISBN 0-9665282-0-4

Acknowledgements

I am thankful to those who helped me picture Homer, Alaska, in the post-World War II era, and to those who read my manuscript and offered words of advice and encouragement. The list would take several pages.

Without Jan O'Meara, her expertise, efficiency, and many kind words and suggestions, this book never would have happened. Thank you, Jan.

A most valuable resource was Elva Scott who lived through many of the experiences of my fictitious characters and who gave me permission to use incidents and information form her book "Homesteading in Homer."

Also thanks to Wilma Williams, who has many memories of this time and place in history, and who has been generous with her time and assistance. I appreciate her giving me permission to use the story about her younger brother "driving" the big six-by-six truck on the beach.

The stories written by the homesteader families for the book, *In Those Days*, were especially helpful. The anecdotes reflected the tone of life in the mid-1940s in Homer.

My profuse "Thank You" to Dianne Widom, who captured my characters and my story so beautifully in her magnificent water colors. Also thanks to my accommodating models for the illustrations, the Haas-Spigelmyer family, especially Katlyn. Thank you a hundred times over, Katlyn, and I hope you like the little girl named Alice as much as I do.

Most of all, I appreciate and thank my husband, Jon, for his advice, tolerance and encouragement, and for listening to me read "Alice" over and over.

This book is dedicated to my grandchildren:
Zeek, Tim, Thomas, Sara Elizabeth
and in loving memory of our angel, Jillian Myra.

Table of Contents

Chapter One
Alice and Her Parents
At the Beach

Alice raced along the gray sandy beach of Kachemak Bay, chasing after the sea gulls that flurried always just beyond her reach. Her parents, Tom and Tide, with several other Homer families, were busy gathering large shiny lumps of coal that had recently washed up on the shore from the coal seams under the bay.

They laughed at Alice's futile efforts with the sea gull chase, as they picked up the coal and filled their big buckets. Using coal as fuel for heating and cooking was not new for the Pennsylvania pioneer family. How-

ever finding and collecting it from the beach of one of the most beautiful bays in the world made the experience novel and exciting.

The adults placed their buckets in a line on the beach as they filled them. When enough buckets stretched out across the firm beach, one of the fathers called to his five-year-old son, "Little Sam! Time to do your job."

Little Sam dropped the big bull kelp seaweed he had been bashing on the beach and ran quickly to his father. He was lifted up onto the seat of the big Army surplus "six by six" truck, geared down to the lowest gear. Sam obviously believed that he was driving, for he seemed puffed up with importance as the truck inched slowly down the beach. The parents and older children hoisted the coal buckets up onto the truck bed as the vehicle moved slowly along. Alice looked on with awe and envy. Little Sam must have felt very grown up and powerful steering that big rig.

Alice had been keeping a journal, written with her own inventive spelling, and that night she wrote about the beach, the snow-capped mountains, the gulls and the shiny coal that seemed cleaner and shinier than the coal from Pennsylvania. She thought about Little Sam and that truck. She picked up her pencil and wrote carefully and thoughtfully:

JUNE 14 WE GT COL FRM TH BECH TU DA
ALASKA COL S SHNY NOT LIK COL AT HOM LTL
SAM GT TU DRIVE TH BG TRK I WD LIK TU DU THT
TU I CHASD GLS ALASKA MTNS HV SNO IN
SUMR

She crossed out the word "home." Snow Shoe, Pennsylvania, was not "home" anymore. The Harrington cabin, in Homer, Alaska, was the temporary home for the Bowmans since they arrived, as it had been for other families who preceded them. The

cabin was rented to newcomers until they could find their own homestead land and construct a cabin.

Alice closed her journal, shut her eyes, and tried to remember how it felt leaving Pennsylvania. She flipped back through her journal to "Day One" and read what she had written.

MAY 5   I M SAD BT HAPE KN I B SD N HAPE BOTH
I MS MARY ND WE AR JST LVNG PNSLVANYA
ALASKA S MNE DAZ AWA

She flipped through some other pages of her journal, and read about the day they got their first flat tire. Did she write about all those other flat tires? Her mother refused to help her "sound out" some of the words her father used after they had more flat tires than a man's patience could handle.

Tide watched Alice as she wrote in her journal, and was pleased that she was as excited about being in Alaska as they were. For Tom and Tide, this had been their big dream since they were in high school together. Their Alaska dream continued as a part of every letter they wrote to each other during the long, drawn out, frightening years of World War II. Tide shuddered, and tried not to think about those anxious days.

Tom had been a pilot of an F-6F on the aircraft carrier *USS Bennington*. Tide's five brothers were all in different branches of "service." She and her mother had kept track of their whereabouts with big world maps tacked up on the dining room wall in their Snow Shoe home. They used a different colored push-pin for each of her five brothers and for her husband, Tom. She located where they were, and had been, in the many different places throughout the United States and the European and Pacific theaters of war.

Tide put away her knitting and gently called to Alice that it was now bedtime. After the long day on

the beach gathering coal, Alice was ready to snuggle into the down-filled sleeping bag her mother had made.

"Let's see, now, where were we?" Tide pretended she had lost the place where the story ended the night before.

"We left off where Tigger and little Roo were throwing pine cones, and Pooh is lost and Tigger is going to help Christopher Robin find Pooh and Roo wants to go, too, but Kanga says 'No', so Christopher Robin and Pooh went off without him," piped Alice.

"You remembered all that!" exclaimed Tide. "How come you can't remember to make up your bed, and put away your clothes?" she asked, laughing.

"That's different 'membering. Read!"

"Read, please, Miss Boss."

"Please, read," Alice corrected.

Tide read a few pages from Alice's favorite book, and not hearing any comments, looked up to realize that her audience was sound asleep. She kissed her and whispered, "Good night, sleepyhead. Pleasant dreams."

Chapter Two
Shangri-La

 Homer was often called "The Shangri-La of Alaska." Shangri-La was the name of a fictitious country that was very beautiful, where everyone was happy, and no-one grew old. Often, a lovely place was referred to as a "Shangri-La."

Tom, Tide and Alice were fascinated by the beauty and bounty of the land around Kachemak Bay, and by the friendliness of the people in Homer. They, too, referred to their new home by the bay as "Shangri-La."

They had driven their army surplus jeep and pulled a trailer containing all their possessions across the United States. They had planned to take the jeep and trailer with them on the *Yukon*, one of the transport ships that carried cargo and people between Seattle, Washington, and ports in Alaska.

Upon arriving in Seattle, the Bowmans discovered there was a pending strike of the dock workers. They were disappointed and discouraged that their long journey should be delayed, but there was little they could do. They were resigned to wait around in the Seattle area for the outcome of the strike threat.

They were walking down a busy Seattle street looking for a place to have lunch before venturing out to find a campground or a hotel room when, suddenly, someone shouted, "Hey, Snow Shoe!"

They all whirled around to see who would be calling out "Snow Shoe" in downtown Seattle. Tom recognized the young man running across the street toward them.

"Gunnison! What the heck are you doing in Seattle?" Tom asked, as the two came together in a bear hug.

"I work here! I live here, remember? But how about you? You are really far from home."

Tom introduced his buddy to Tide and Alice. Gunnison took Tide's hand and said, "I am so happy to meet you. Tom talked about you and this lady, Alice, all the time, and we were all jealous that he had you to think about and to get home to." He took Alice's small hand in his, kneeled down in front of her, and gallantly kissed her hand. Alice giggled.

"You are a lucky lady to have this guy for a dad, Alice. He was the best pilot we had on the *Bennington.*"

He stood and put his arm around Tom's shoulder and said, "Old pal of mine, what are you doing on the streets of Seattle?"

Tom told him about their well-planned trip to Homer, Alaska, that was now stymied by the pending dock strike. They were resigned to spend time in Seattle to wait for the cargo ship to take them to Homer.

"Well, just like the luck you always had on some of those hairy missions we flew, you are in luck now, old buddy of mine, because you know what? I am chief pilot of a big cargo plane that is flying some equipment up to that mining operation outside of Fairbanks. The equipment isn't very big or very heavy, it's just something they have to have, immediately. They can't remain shut down waiting for this dock strike that is threatening to delay everything. So, they chartered this plane to get the part up to the mine. We stop in Anchorage to refuel, and we have space for that rig I see over there, and for you and your pretty ladies. Not the loveliest of seating accommodations, but, hey, we will get you part of the way there. There are small cargo planes that fly to Homer. What do you say?"

"What can we say, but thanks to you and to whatever powers brought you and the three of us together on this street at this time! I flew to Homer in a small cargo plane before. There is no road down there, you know. Let's have lunch and think about this! Do we have time?"

"The very place I was headed," laughed Gunnison. "If I remember correctly, the last time I saw you, you were such a penny pincher, I had to buy you lunch, then, too."

"Our turn to spring for your lunch, Gunny. You never could remember important things, but when it came to filling that stomach, your memory never failed."

They walked down the street together, laughing and reminiscing about a shared past and future prospects. After lunch, the Bowmans followed Gunnison out to the airport to check out the huge cargo plane that was all loaded for the Alaska flight. Gunnison and Tom talked with others about the possible means to complete the odyssey of the Bowman family to Homer. Tom felt confident that they would locate the same plane and pilot that he used on his initial trip.

The jeep and trailer were loaded according to Gunnison's orders, and three seats were pulled down from the side of the plane for Alice, Tide and Tom. Alice went into the cockpit and was speechless as she gazed at all the dials and instruments.

She looked up at Tom and asked, "Did your F6F plane look like this, Daddy, with all these clocks?"

"Not quite," Tom said, laughing, "but something like that."

They arrived in Anchorage hours later. They were tired, but exhilarated, after the long bumpy flight. Although they had flown over breathtakingly beautiful mountains and water, the passengers were unable to see them, since the windows were at their backs.

At the Anchorage airport, after the jeep and trailer were unloaded, Gunnison and Tom talked with some of the ground crew about transports to Homer. The crew knew about, and recommended, the same small cargo plane that Tom took when he went to Homer to explore the prospects of living there.

Thank yous, farewells and promises to keep in touch were exchanged with Gunnison, then they watched him and his plane go down the runway and soar off toward Fairbanks. A tip of the wings was his farewell. The three weary travelers set out with one of the ground crew to find the other cargo plane.

Lady Luck was with them again! They were taken to a hangar and met the pilot, who remembered Tom. He said he could take them down to Homer the next day, if the weather stayed favorable, but they would have to make two trips. The plane could not take both the trailer and the jeep, plus three passengers.

They decided to take the trailer and the family first, then the jeep could be brought down on another flight.

The pilot reminded Tom that the Homer airstrip left a lot to be desired, but the weather had been good and the runway wouldn't be too boggy. The Bowmans made arrangements with the pilot to meet at the airport the next day. The cost of the two flights was quite expensive. Tom and Alice did a quick calculation of the amounts budgeted for the boat and meals for the three of them and probably a hotel and meals in Seattle waiting for the *Yukon.* They decided that they were not too far over budget — besides, they had few choices.

The weary, but excited trio spent the night in a small hotel, and the next day they flew off to Homer with their packed trailer in the small cargo plane.

In Homer, they readily found help getting their trailer hauled into town to the store that Tom remembered as the town's "hub" for information and assistance. There, they found out that the Harrington cabin was available for rent and that they could move in immediately. They purchased white flour, whole wheat flour and sugar in one-hundred-pound sacks, a case

of canned milk, and other necessities such as salt, pepper and lard. Tide resisted buying "boat eggs," as the locals called the eggs that were shipped by boat to Alaska. Boat eggs had a rotten odor and equally bad taste. They piled their purchases into a borrowed cart and headed over to the cabin.

People seemed to appear out of nowhere, introduced themselves and promptly helped to unload the trailer. Soon, someone came with a big pot of moose stew, some homemade bread, and a rhubarb pie for their evening meal. Others came with a load of wood and coal and started a fire in the cabin stove. The Bowmans learned about genuine Alaskan hospitality on their first day in Homer.

"However do we thank you all?" Tide asked.

"You just did," replied one of the women. "This is Alaska, and this is how we do things here. I look forward to seeing you, again, real soon."

The Bowmans had arrived! They were ecstatic about what they were seeing and learning. They walked around town often, exploring and checking out the Homer library, two churches, two general stores, the cold-storage locker plant, two small sawmills, cannery and the school. Alice was especially interested in the school, which was a large white building with dormer windows on the top floor. They were told that the new principal-teacher lived there.

They drove their jeep on all the negotiable public roads in the area, looked at homes and planned what they would build. Alice, fascinated by the meat caches that she saw, voted to have a cache built first, so she could use it as a playhouse and a lookout. They were pleased to see the flourishing gardens of Homer, and astonished to see the native grasses that grew over six feet tall. They were told that almost everything could be grown in Homer. The rich soil, the mild climate, and the extended growing time of the long summer days of sunshine made the area an ideal site for gardens.

People grew most of their own vegetables, picked berries, ate halibut, salmon, king crab, clams, mussels, moose, bear, rabbit and ptarmigan. For fuel, they had wood on their own property and coal they could gather from beaches and from the coal veins on their own land.

Such a paradise. It was Shangri-La, indeed.

At night, after Alice was asleep, Tom and Tide loved to prop their feet up on the oven door of the wood- and coal-burning stove in their rented cabin. They talked about conversations they had with people in town. They discussed what they were learning about the community and, perhaps more importantly, what the community seemed to be learning about them. Everyone knew that Tom, the handsome naval aviator, had returned after his brief visit to Homer, immediately after his discharge from the service. They knew he hoped to make a claim for a 160-

13

acre homestead parcel. They also knew that Tide was a school teacher in Pennsylvania, and was interested in being a substitute teacher or a tutor.

Although the Harrington cabin was a pleasant place to stay, the Bowmans were anxious to get to work on their own land and to start the process of building. Tom unpacked all his tools and lined them up along the cabin wall: saws, axes, hammers, wedges, planes and all other manner of carpentry tools. He rubbed them with oil, sharpened the blades, and obviously ached to put them to use building his own house.

Chapter Three
Meeting Some Neighbors
Making Some Friends

 Early one morning, after breakfast, Tom went off, as usual, to look at land for their homestead. Alice and her mother got ready to go for a walk along the path behind the cabin. They packed some sandwiches and juice for a picnic. Dangling from their belts were two berry buckets, just in case they found some bushes waiting to be picked.

Alice had a special rag doll, named Becky, that she was packing up to go along on the walk. Becky was a stocking doll that her grandmother had made for her from a big white sock. She had a ruffled white skirt held fast by a big, shiny, many-faceted, ruby-red button that Alice had selected from her Grandmother Lizabeth's button box.

Alice stuffed Becky into one of the buckets, but the doll's chubby legs stuck up in the air. Becky kept popping out as Alice hurried after her mother. Alice stopped and sat down on the grassy path to push and stuff Becky back down into the bucket. She found some interesting stones on the path, which she plunked in her bucket. She chattered and fussed with her doll, and was in her own small world. Then suddenly she heard her mother's

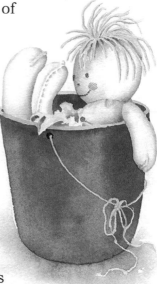

scream, "Alice! Alice!"

The call was filled with fear and was not her mother's usual tone when she called to her. Alice leaped up to look for her mother, but she could not see anything over the tall alder trees along the path.

"Alice! Alice ! Answer me!"

"Mommy, I'm here!" Alice yelled back, as she ran down the path. Tears streamed down her face, and her heart pounded wildly in her chest.

"Mommy, Mommy!"

Becky popped out of the bucket again, and Alice stooped down to retrieve her. The string on the bucket broke and the bucket clattered across the stones. Alice picked it up and ran on, clanging the two buckets together.

Alice heard her mother's shouts coming closer and closer. Then, suddenly, a dark shadow crossed the path in front of her. She looked up and gasped as she saw a big, shiny, black bear, standing up on its hind legs looking at her.

Alice screamed louder and, in her hysteria, clanged the two buckets together faster and louder. The bear dropped down on all fours and ran into the woods, and was soon lost from sight in the thick alders. Tide came running down the path, swooped her little girl up into her arms and hugged her so tightly, Alice could scarcely breathe. Alice's face was wet and messy with tears.

Tide swayed back and forth, back and forth, hugging tighter and tighter, sobbing and mumbling over and over, "Oh, my baby, oh my baby. I could have lost you." Slowly the swaying and sobbing stopped, and the two slid slowly down to the ground. They sat with legs tangled together for a moment just looking at each other, searching each other's faces with their eyes.

Alice was the first to speak through her sobs. "Mommy, I'm so sorry. I didn't know. I didn't know. I

didn't know — the bear — the bear — Becky kept plopping out of my bucket and I had to push her back in. I didn't know you were not right there in front of me. I'm sorry, Mommy. I'm so sorry I scared you. I'm sorry I forgot I can't never let me out of your sight."

Tide wiped the tears from her own face and cleaned and kissed Alice's dirty, tear-streaked face, saying, "I am the one who should be saying I am sorry to you, Alice.

"We cannot assume that we are safe on paths around our house. We are not back in Grandma 'Lizabeth's back yard, anymore. We had ourselves one big scare, and we learned one enormous lesson. But, you know what? I'll bet that big old bear was more scared than we were, especially with those silly old berry buckets clanging like a fire engine, and me screaming like a banshee."

"What's a banshee, Mommy?"

"I have no idea, but I guess they're people who scream a lot when they're scared."

Tide mussed Alice's hair, laughed and said, "I suppose I will have to help you sound out banshee for your journal writing tonight."

"Yep. I like that word—banshee. Were they good people or bad people?"

"You got me there, little one. I have no idea what they were. But I like to think that they were good people who had some things to scream about. Let's go, now."

As they stood up from where they were sitting on the grassy path, they heard voices and a faint jingling sound coming toward them. Alice clutched her mother's hand and ducked behind her.

Peering out around her mother's leg, Alice saw three little girls skipping and hopping toward them. Around the bend of the tree-lined path, behind the girls, came two women, smiling and waving to Tide

18

and Alice. Two of the children appeared to be about Alice's age. The smallest of the girls smiled at her and quietly asked, "Did the bear hurt you?"

Alice looked at her, shaking her head "no" in answer to her question. She was thrilled to see girls her size. She was enchanted with the jingling she was hearing as the girls moved along the path toward her. She soon discovered they all had tiny bells tied around their ankles.

"I like your bells," Alice ventured.

"We wear them to warn the bears that people are coming, so the bears can get out of the way and not get shot."

"I am Helen Haynes, and this is my daughter, Susan, my sister, Shirley McKinley, and her daughters, Diane and Sybil. We have already heard a lot about you."

"I am delighted to meet you" Tide said, smiling. "My name is Tide Bowman, and this is Alice, who just met her first bear."

"Not a fun way to get introduced to Alaska, is it Alice? We saw it thrashing through the trees," Shirley offered.

"Diane and Susan will be in first grade this year, how about you?" asked Helen.

A meek "Me, too" was all Alice could offer, as she nudged closer to her mother.

The youngest little girl, named Sybil, was not old enough for school, but she was not at all shy, nor at a loss for words. She needed to know all about the doll, Becky, and she asked why she had that red, shiny button on her dress. She chattered away about her doll, Pearly.

Everyone was so excited about new friends with bells on their ankles and black bears standing between Alice and her mother, that no one seemed to be listening to anyone else. That did not bother Sybil. She chattered to anyone who would pretend to listen as the group walked back up the path in the direction from which the five had come. Alice and Tide were invited to join them for lunch at the McKinleys' cabin. They enjoyed their visit with their new friends, and learned that the Haynes family lived quite a distance away, on another homestead plot. They also learned that both families fished, farmed and loved Alaska, especially Homer.

Before Alice and Tide left, Helen insisted that they take some freshly made jams, bread, and smoked salmon home with them. She also added some fresh berries for a pie, since the bear had cheated them out of a chance to pick berries.

The two families insisted on going back down the path with Alice and her mother until they were well past the spot where Mr. Bear used to be. Alice was pleased about that, and she walked along, pressed closely to her mother's leg and hanging on tightly to her hand. Although all the others were walking, jingling, and talking, seemingly without fear, Alice was still gun-shy or rather, "bear-shy".

After their new friends said goodbye and turned around to go back to their cabin, Tide felt Alice stiffen with fear. She stooped down in front of her, and looked at her pale face.

"You've had enough trauma today to last a year, my little lady. Climb on my back and wrap your legs tightly around my waist. If you get too heavy for me, we will stop and rest."

Alice did as her mother asked, and they started back down the path toward home. Their buckets, stuffed with small stones, jam jars, bread, salmon and berries dangled and clanged as the walked. They made quite a scene, as well as a great racket.

If Alice was aware that her favorite little rag doll, Becky, with the shiny red button on her dress, was not

among the cans and jars on this trip home, she gave no inkling. She nestled her face into her mother's neck and kept her legs wrapped tightly around her waist. She blinked hard to keep from falling asleep.

Alice heard someone or something approaching. She tensed, and then, with great relief, saw her father heading up the path toward them. He quickened his step as he saw Alice on her mother's back. Both Alice and her mother yelled, "Helloooo," at the same time.

Tide stooped down and Alice leaped off her back and ran to Tom. He swooped her up, and shook her gently and lovingly up in the air above his head.

"You had me scared, at first. I thought you were hurt, Button-nose, but now I see you were just a lazy little hitch-hiker."

He squatted down, and Alice leaped on his back and hugged him so hard that her arms and legs ached from the "good squeezing" she gave him.

Tide and Alice regaled Tom with their exciting adventures with the bear and meeting new friends. He tried not to show the fear that he felt.

Tom had exciting news to share about the possibility of a homestead plot that might be available, but he felt it almost paled in comparison to their day of adventure.

That night, they got ready for bed early, after they shared with one another more details of their adventurous day. Alice got out her journal and wrote:

TU DA WZ THE SKREST DA UV MI LIF IF I HV MNE
MOR DAZE LIK TU DA I MA ASK TU GO BK TU
GRNMA LIZBTH ALASKA S A SKRE PLAS MABE I
WL GT ME SM BLS FR MY FET I LRND ABT A
BANCHE TU DA

The bedtime story started out as a story of a screaming banshee who lost his shoes and was screaming because his feet hurt, but soon became a story about a banshee who turned into a screaming bear. They tried to out-do each other with silly jokes and story lines. All three were giggling and snickering, each trying to be sillier than the other.

Tom had everyone feeling sorry for that poor scared, defenseless bear. The poor fellow was out there trying to figure out what kind of creatures clanged berry picking cans and screamed like banshees. Tide had the bear turning into a Prince Charming, hoping that the beautiful Alice would come back soon. They joked about drinking the "beary" juice that Helen gave them and about what happens to people who eat "beary" pie.

"What kind of pies do 'bearies' eat?"

"Not 'beary', surely."

"What about 'beary' jam?"

"Was that 'beary' toe jam?"

"How about 'beary' jammies? Wouldn't they be 'furry' nice and warm?"

Alice giggled and tried to out-do the "beary" bad bear stories from her parents. She was giggling so hard she was soon sleeping with little "hics" of laughter. A smile was on her lips; she showed no obvious sign of fear about bears.

Tide and Tom had been too preoccupied with the tales of adventure, the supper and clean-up chores to notice the absence of Alice's good friend and traveling companion, soft, huggable Becky. There had been no word from Alice about the loss of the doll. Both parents realized, at the same time, that constant companion Becky was not in Alice's arm as she slept, looking like an angel in her colorful sleeping bag.

"We will worry about all that tomorrow," Tom said. "We have done enough work and worry for one day, and had more excitement in eighteen hours than most people have in their lifetimes."

The following day Alice wrote in her journal:

23

BK S GN I WL I NVR SE HR AGN I M SO SD MABE
THE BR GT HR WUD THE BR ET HR HUL KN I TL
GRNMA LIZBTH

Weeks went by with the Bowmans making new
friends and adjusting to life in Homer. Just when Tom
was feeling a little discouraged about land prospects,
the awaited miracle happened. Tom was told they
could get a 160-acre homestead out east of town, if
they were able to "prove up" on it. Since Tom was a
veteran, they did not need to clear trees or plant crops.
They just had to build a habitable house and live in it
for at least seven months to "prove up."
    They walked all over the land as soon as they got
the word. They were thrilled with the possibilities it
offered. The homestead was located east of town on a
mildly sloping piece of land on the south side of what
barely qualified as a road. The land sloped down to the
bay, where a narrow beach was accessible by climbing
down a small cliff. There were enough trees on the
homestead plot for felling and building a small cabin.
    Tom had met and talked with many of the men in
the community who were ready to help when they got
the word from him. It was now the end of June, and
three and a half months was a short time to complete
all they would need to do.

Chapter Four
Sybil Solves a Mystery

 Tom left early one morning for the homestead. He took along three of the men who would help him clear, select trees to cut for logs, and erect a small cabin as quickly as possible. They would be able to help him throughout the summer, whenever they found time from their own busy survival chores.

Tide and Alice had long lists of things that they needed to do, also. On this beautiful, sunny day, they were on their way to the McKinley cabin in the woods. Alice was anxious to see Diane and Sybil again. Today, she had her own set of bells tied securely to her ankles, and she skipped, high-stepped and jumped to make them jingle.

The three families enjoyed getting together to go beach combing, fishing and hiking. The most fascinating event for Alice was watching Mr. McKinley haul up a huge king-crab pot out of the bay, with an enormous crab in it. Later, he threw the crab into a big kettle of boiling sea water. Watching it turn from a dull tan to a beautiful red color was amazing to Alice. Best of all was cracking and eating the crab. She licked her lips, remembering the taste of melted butter and the sweet, sweet chunks of crab meat.

Their mission this day was to can some of the salmon they had smoked in the McKinley smokehouse. Since Tide had not yet unpacked her big canner, she had to use Shirley McKinley's canner. She bought some new jars at the store and had them wrapped carefully in towels and shirts in a laundry bag slung over her shoulder. Alice's job was to carry the lunch in her homemade backpack, strapped on her back.

As they were walking and jingle-jangling down the path, a bright red light in a tree caught Tide's eye. It blinked, then it was gone.

"Whatever can that be?" she asked out loud.

"Whatever can what be?" echoed Alice.

"Up there on that branch in the tree." Tide stooped down beside Alice pointing up toward a tree taller than the surrounding alders.

"I can't see anything 'cept trees," Alice answered, squinting into all the trees where her mother was pointing.

"There! I saw it again. See that mess of twigs up there on that branch? Follow where I am pointing. A red light blinks and then is gone." Alice scrunched up her eyes and tried to see what it was her mother was seeing.

"Alice, I know what it is!" exclaimed Tide.

Tide went to the line of alders along the path and through them to a tall birch swaying slightly in the light breeze. Tide pulled slowly and steadily on the supple branch, then she beckoned to Alice to come over to the tree.

Alice parted the alder branches and stood on her tiptoes to look up into the trees.

She squealed, "Becky! Becky! Oh, my Becky! How did you get up there?"

Her mother shook the branch, and Becky came flying out. Alice retrieved her as soon as she hit the ground. She hugged the doll tightly, and then held her out at arm's length to check her over.

"Her button, Mommy, that's what you saw."

Tide came back out to the path where Alice was holding the rag doll with the ruby-red button sewn tightly on her dress front. They sat down in the grassy path and admired their find.

"Alice, how do you think Becky got up in that tree?"

"Some bad person threw her up there." Alice scowled, fingering some small holes she was discovering on Becky's dress front.

"Is that what you really think?" inquired Tide.

"That's what I really think," Alice mumbled.

"That's not what I think." Tide smiled, and held Alice's hands as she cradled the soiled, damaged sock doll.

"Look at those holes. What might have made those holes? What would you need to poke those funny little holes in Becky?"

"A knife?" ventured Alice, quietly.

"Do you think some bad person poked holes in her and threw her up there in that branch?"

Alice made no reply, but she turned her floppy doll over and over in an attempt to find answers to her mother's questions somewhere on the doll. Finally, after much turning and pondering she looked up into her mother's face and said in a very small voice, "You tell me."

Tide stood up and pulled Alice up beside her. She gathered their bags and bundles together and continued up the path. Alice tagged along behind, still staring at Becky, then ran to get in step with her mother.

"You tell me," she repeated.

Tide reached down and took her hand and replied, "You need to figure this out. You need to be a good detective and figure out this mystery."

Alice trudged along beside her mother, still holding Becky out in front of her and staring . Her brow was furrowed in thought.

They were soon in sight of the McKinleys' cabin and Alice still had not been able to give voice to this wonderment. This funny, little floppy doll, that she loved so much, disappeared the first day she and her mother came up this path, and Alice had not been able to talk about it. She cried at night softly to herself after her mother and father tucked her in bed. She had substituted a buckwheat-stuffed "Winnie the Pooh" bear that her grandmother also made. Sometimes, the bear was placed in the oven for a while before bedtime. The warmed buckwheat had a sweet smell and the bear became a great bed warmer. Sometimes he was relegated to the foot of the bed to warm Alice's toes.

Occasionally, Tide and Tom would talk about the doll and speculate how she could possibly disappear from everyone's scrutiny. The McKinleys searched high and low, but found no trace of Becky. Now, here she was, back safely.

Tide was as eager as Alice to show their friends the doll with the mysterious small holes in it.

Sybil had kept a vigil all morning long, hoping to see Alice first. She came flying down the path to greet them, and stopped mid-flight when she saw Becky. She shrieked, wheeled around and ran back to the cabin, shouting, "She's back! She's back! She's back!"

All the McKinleys, plus Susan and Helen Haynes, came running to see what all the clamor was about. Each gasped when they saw Alice standing there with arms straight out in front of her, with Becky clutched in her hands, as if she were some sacred offering to the gods.

As was their custom, the McKinleys and Haynes all started talking at once, and it was difficult to hear what was being said, except that the conversations all focused on Becky the doll.

As Becky was being passed around, Tide told the story about the red light that she saw at the top of the birch tree. Each person then took turns stating how she thought Becky got twenty feet up in a birch tree.

The adults enjoyed giving preposterous suggestions when their turns came. Sybil was being very pensive and never took her eyes off Becky. Her turn came last, and she solemnly and quietly muttered, so softly that everyone strained forward to listen.

"I think that some greedy old bird wanted that red button, and when Alice wasn't looking, the nasty bird flew down and snatched that little doll up in the air by her little red button. And that bird wanted her baby birds to have that doll with the red button. That's what I think."

Everyone cheered, and again, everyone was talking and no one was listening. Alice went over to Sybil and put her arm around her shoulders and guided her out onto the porch.

The two little girls sat down together on the edge of the porch, and neither said a word for a long time. The adults held Diane and Susan back, and whispered to them that they should just stay inside for a while.

Alice's journal entry that night read:

BKE S BK I KN TL GRAMS LIZBTH A BRD TUK
HR WN I WS NOT LUKNG BUT SHE S BK

Chapter Five
A Special Grandma

Alice was busy with her assigned job for the morning. She was dragging small branches over to the side of the cleared property and piling them up in a big heap. Later, when it was safe to have a fire, Tom would burn the discarded branches.

Her next duty was to gather three baskets of moss that would be used to stuff between the logs of the cabin, to keep the cabin snug. After that task was completed she was off duty, and could climb up the ladder into the meat cache to play. The cache was built first for a safe place for Alice while all adults were busy sawing trees, shaving bark, piling logs, and doing numerous other tasks.

Up in her cache, Alice had her journal, crayons, and an old Sears catalog from which she cut out paper doll families. Her buddy, Becky, who had major surgery and a new dress, was always with her. The cache had a large opening through which Alice could look out at three gleaming blue and white glaciers and the startling white, snow-capped mountains surrounding them. The bay was always changing color and reflecting the clouds and the sun. She felt as if she could see forever. She sometimes mused that this must be what Heaven looks like.

Alice thumbed through her journal and read what she had written the night before:

JUNE 21,
I SLEP N DA TIM I MS SE EN STRS
IN WNTR THR R STRS IN ALASKA I GS
WY S ALASKA ALWAYS DA TIM IN SUMR

She rummaged through her pencil box and found a

pencil to record the good and lofty feelings she now had:

JUNE 22,

I M UP SO HI I KN SE 4 EVR

CLUDS GLASHRS MONTNS BA

While Alice played in her cache, Tide and Tom worked on the cabin. Tide was able to do almost all the things that a man could do, except for very heavy lifting. The summer seemed unusually hot, and there was not much rainfall. Weather had become the major subject for conversation in the community.

The Bowmans, newcomers to the land of the midnight sun, frequently commented on how unusual it was not to have a regular dark night and a bright day to give one a sense of time. Often when they became a little cranky and short tempered, Tide realized with good humor that it was several hours past their usual dinner hour and well past Alice's bedtime.

The work on the buildings progressed well. Besides Alice's private penthouse — the meat cache — there was a shed made for storing the tools, the foundation work for the cabin was finished, and the outhouse had become a work of art. No other outdoor facility in the world could possibly have a view as magnificent.

The McKinley and Haynes families insisted that Tide and Tom should stop working so hard and observe the Fourth of July as a national holiday, just like everyone else. Along with the new school principal, Gene Haduch, and his wife, Margie, and Herb and Jane Confer and all their children, they hiked in one mile to Diamond Creek. They fished in the cold, clear rippling water of Diamond Creek for trout. The fresh trout, cooked over the campfire on the beach, was added to the bountiful picnic lunches they had packed in and shared with one another. The wide beach stretched along sixty-foot cliffs, and the low tide provided a wide expanse of packed sand for games for both adults and children. They could see beautiful Mt.

Illiamna and Mt. St. Augustine clearly in the distance, across the sparkling water.

Alice raced, played and laughed with her best friends, Diane, Susan and Sybil. She met Lori Confer and Kermit Haduch, who were also her age and would be in her class at school in the fall. There were people of all ages laughing and playing together on the beach.

While the families were eating their lunch, Alice asked when there would be fireworks.

She was very embarrassed when adults and older children laughed and reminded her that you cannot see a fireworks display in broad daylight. A friendly grandmother put her arm around Alice and said, "We save our fireworks for our New Year's celebration. That way we can see them against the dark sky. I will make sure that you are rousted out of bed to see how beautiful Alaska fireworks can be, on New Year's eve."

Alice appreciated the warm hug and the soft words. This grandmother reminded her a lot of her own grandmother back in Pennsylvania. The same soft, silver hair, the twinkle in her eyes, and the way

she laughed and smiled, especially with children.

The grandmother leaned close to Alice, and asked, "What is your name again? I heard it once but with all these little ones around, I am not remembering all their names."

"My name is Alice Elizabeth Bowman. My

mother is Tide. It's really Myra, but when she was little her nickname was 'Midey,' but her baby brother couldn't say 'Midey.' He said 'Tidey,' and she has been called that all her life. My daddy is Tom Bowman. I had two grandmothers in Pennsylvania, Grandma Bowman and Grandma Bland. Grandma Bowman died a long time ago, before I was born. I lived with my Grandma 'Lizbeth."

She rattled on, delivering more family history. Then she suddenly stopped chatting and asked, "What is your name? Are you a grandma?"

Laughing, the older woman replied, "You can call me Grandma Char."

Tide looked over at Alice snuggling closer to Mrs. Montague, and at the two chatting away. Soon Alice got up and came over to where her mother was sitting and announced, "I have a Grandma Char here in Homer, now. She said Pennsylvania was too far away to get good hugs from Grandma 'Lizbeth. So she is going to be my Alaska good-hugging grandma."

Tears filled Tide's eyes, and she smiled at Char Montague across the campfire and mouthed the words, "Thank you so much." She missed her own mother, and knew Alice felt the same emptiness at times.

The picnickers started packing up to go back to town. They were all going to see the movie that was playing that night. After the movies some hearty, party people were also going to the Fourth of July dance, complete with live music. Walking back up along the beautiful sparkling Diamond Creek, Alice made her way over beside her newly found grandma and walked along with her, chatting away. Tom leaned over and quietly asked Tide, "What family secrets do you suppose Mrs. Montague is getting from our little girl, now?"

Tide, laughed and whispered back, "Maybe she is telling her that we are wicked, wicked people who have kidnapped her from her real parents."

"She's capable of that." Tom chuckled.

34

Chapter Six
A New Member Of The Family

 One of the first great finds for the Bowmans was a beautiful young Siberian Husky/ Newfoundland dog named Petey Joe. He was a gift from a family who went back to Oregon. They could scarcely afford to pay fare for their family of five, much less a dog. The farewell was sad, because the children loved Petey Joe so much.

Luckily for Petey Joe, he got a kid who was homesick for her beagle, Nellie, back in Pennsylvania.

Petey Joe was truly a special gift, for he loved children, and he became a constant companion for Alice. He was frustrated at first when Alice retreated to her meat-cache penthouse. He lay down at the base of the cache and refused to move until Alice would come down to join him.

Petey Joe proved to be a great hunter and provider, as well as nanny for Alice. He could spot a moose long before anyone else noticed it, but he had been trained not to chase them. He just stood and stared in the direction the moose were browsing. Bears were a different matter. He barked and yelped, but kept a safe distance. Alice insisted upon having some little bells attached to Petey Joe's collar, just for extra insurance with the bears.

Petey Joe sat staring at a beautiful bull moose one day, at the base of the hill from the cache. He went over to Tom and nudged his knee. Tom reached down and petted him, but Petey Joe kept bumping Tom's knee with his long nose. Tom became perturbed at the nuisance, until Queen Alice bellowed down from her lofty cache, "Look! Look! Daddy. The moose with the huge horns!"

Tom, Charley, Phil and the other men helping Tom with the cabin quickly spotted the magnificent bull moose. The old-timers among them estimated his age, and concluded he was young enough to be very tender, indeed.

Alice had a tough time with the shooting, but she was not pampered. She was told that all her ancestors had grown strong and healthy eating the venison from the Pennsylvania woods, and if she stayed in Alaska she would be expected to hunt moose along with her parents.

The hanging and gutting of the moose fascinated her. Full of curiosity, she would poke at blobby things in the offal with a stick and ask what they were.

"So that's what my heart looks like," she exclaimed. She continued poking through the innards, learning about the other parts of the creature.

Alice was an important part of the moose-canning operation, back at the cabin in town. Her small hand was just the right size to push the chunks of meat firmly into the jars.

Petey Joe made another great find on the homestead plot. Tide and Alice were hiking through the tall grassy plain, and Petey Joe was bounding along ahead of them. The day was beautiful, not a cloud in the sky, and the temperatures were reported to be in the mid-eighties. Alice had on some shorts and a cool top Tide had made for her to wear on these hot, sunny days. She was so tan, she looked more like a California beach girl than a Cheechako, or newcomer to Alaska.

Petey Joe stopped abruptly, just ahead of them in the path. He pawed around in the grasses a few times and then they heard him lapping up water. Tide realized he had found a spring or an underground stream that had come very close to the surface. She was excited about their find, or rather Petey Joe's find.

She got down on her knees and cleared away the

grasses where Petey Joe had been drinking. The water gushed up out of the ground after being freed of the strangling grasses. Tide found a few stones and asked Alice to search for some more. While Tide busied herself building a little stone basin around the bubbling water, Alice and Petey Joe went bounding off in search of some more stones.

A loud, piercing scream came from the direction Alice had gone. Tide leaped up and ran over and saw

Alice dancing up and down in a frenzy. Her legs were pumping, and she was frantically rubbing her bare arms as if to get rid of some crawling insects. The screams became louder as Tide reached her. Tide picked Alice up, still screaming and rubbing her arms and legs. Tide looked around where she found Alice. She discovered a large patch of plants that she guessed must be what someone had described to her as stinging nettles.

She carried Alice, who was still shrieking and squirming, back to the spring and plunged her into the puddle of water that welled up in the stone dam. She splashed the cold water over the reddening skin on Alice's bare arms and legs. She yelled to Petey Joe, who came running back to see what all the commotion was about. She pointed in the direction of the cabin building project and shouted to the dog, "Go! Go! Petey Joe! Go get Tom."

That marvelous beast sensed exactly what the command meant, and was off through the grasses in a flash. Tide continued splashing Alice and took off her own shirt, soaked it in the cold spring water to wrap around Alice's legs, then re-soaked the shirt and wrapped the arms. Alice was just whimpering, now, and there was an occasional sob.

Tom came running down the path, with Petey Joe leading the way through the trampled grass. Close behind were Charley Haynes and another man Tide did not know.

"Yi! Nettles!" Charley said when he saw the little red dots on Alice's arm. "I'd be screaming, too, Alice." He gently nudged Tom and Petey Joe aside and squatted down beside Alice and Tide.

"Oddly enough, Alice, the best cure for nettle rash is a gentle rub with more nettles. Where were you when you got into them?"

"Over there," Alice pointed, trembling.

Charley went in the direction Alice had pointed and soon came back with stalks of nettles held in his shirt, which he had shed.

He got down beside Alice again and said, "Now this may be a little scary, but this is what we have to do. I rub these fresh nettles in the cloth like this, then I will have to rub the crushed nettles on your rash. O.K.?"

"O.K." Alice consented, still trembling.

Charley gently rubbed the crushed nettles on the little legs and arms, while Tide and Tom stood by transfixed and unable to say anything.

"Like cures like," mumbled Tom. "Your aunt, the homeopathic nurse, told us that, Tide."

The welts that had formed on Alice's' legs and arms were vanishing and she was much calmer.

"Dock and fiddle fern, that scruff part of them is a

cure, too," Charley said. Then to Alice, "Are you O.K. now, Alice scrum Dalice?"

He smiled and Alice smiled back, nodding her head.

"Well, now that we are here, what is this little grotto we're looking at?" Tom asked.

"This little grotto is our water source, I believe," boasted Tide. "But I can't take any credit for it, because the same family member who first saw the moose that has fed four families, and the same family member who obeys a command to 'get Tom' when we are in danger is the exact same family member who found a spring."

"And nettles," mumbled Alice.

"Actually, Alice, those nettles are one of the best foods you can find in Alaska," Charley said, "We'll get you some recipes, Tide. Talk to Shirley and Helen. They put them in everything you can think of: soup, salad, bread, and just served alone as a vegetable. They're great. They have some of those goatskin garden gloves that they use when they go after nettles. You folks have the best vegetable garden right here for the picking."

Alice, now cured of the stinging nettles, seemed a little proud to think that she was the one who discovered the nettles, painful though they were.

In the succeeding days of summer, the cabin walls were going up fast. Tom and Tide enjoyed a great deal of help from their many newfound friends in the community. They had set a goal to have the two stories up before August 1, but now they had the attitude, "maybe we'll make it, and maybe we won't."

They took time to do other things, such as explore across the bay with new friends who invited them to go in their boat. Alice was amazed at the creatures she found in the tidal pools. She wanted to collect everything that she saw, but Tom told her that the living things must be put back in their homes. Old shells were all right to collect, but not the living things.

The Bowmans had picnics with other families in a beautiful little wooded copse on the spit of land that jutted about four miles out into the bay. Everyone referred to the area as Green Timbers. Alice now knew over a dozen children who would be in the elementary school with her. She knew five who would be in her class.

Tide and Alice met often with the McKinley and the Haynes families to can berries, vegetables, rhubarb, salmon, halibut, crab, clams, and to make jams and jellies. They even made sauerkraut in huge crocks.

The berries were so plentiful, they had more than they needed. They learned that a woman had just started a business making and selling wild berry jams and jellies. She was buying from anyone who had more berries than they could use. The three families saw an opportunity to earn some extra cash, so they took fifteen to twenty buckets down every day, and divided the money equally among all seven berry pickers.

Alice never had money of her own, before, except for a penny, nickel or dime, occasionally, that someone gave her for a treat. She kept looking at things in Mrs.Walter's store, thinking about what her money could buy, but she would never spend any. Sybil, on the other hand, was rapidly going into debt by borrowing from her older, wiser sister, Diane, whenever she saw something she liked in the store.

Chapter Seven
A Welcome Stranger

 Tom quietly got out of bed, dressed in his work clothes, grabbed a loaf of bread, some coffee, a jar of canned salmon, and headed out to the homestead early. He needed time by himself without any interference to think through what needed to be done and in what order. The family needed to move into their own cabin and get settled. He needed to plan what his future might be in this small town. He yearned to get into a cockpit again and feel the power and thrill of soaring through space. He did not think when he was discharged that he would miss flying that much, even though he had signed up for the Reserves.

As he thought about Homer and Alaska on this beautiful August morning, driving out to an unfinished cabin in Shangri-La, he wanted to pat himself on the back for forethought and perseverance. He loved all he saw here, and he knew Tide loved the place and Alice would grow up in a safe little town, just as he and Tide had done. He realized that he was going to need something more than just hunting, fishing, chopping wood and shoveling snow, but what that something was he could not yet perceive.

Tom had no regrets about their decision to come to Alaska, and homesteading was sort of fun — hard work, yes — but still fun and challenging. He had been monitoring carefully all their expenses and projected costs and knew he still had time to explore employment possibilities before the funds ran out. He marveled silently about the people in Homer who had only a few dollars more than their transportation up here. They seemed content with their lot and obviously were

41

doing all right by picking up jobs here and there. He remained convinced that Alaska had a great future and that there was a role for him and his family here.

He was still deep in his thoughts when he turned the jeep into the homestead. He was startled to see a small fire burning in the fire ring and a very large form sitting by the fire. He got out of the jeep and walked over to the ring, as the uninvited guest stood up and extended a hand the size of a small ham.

Tom shook the proffered hand, and said, "I don't think I've seen you around before. You must be new to Homer. I am Tom Bowman, and this is my land you're on."

"Nope, you haven't seen me around. I just came in yesterday. My name is Karl Gray, but most people in Alaska know me as Moose."

"Now, why would anyone call you that?" Tom chuckled, as he looked up at the huge man across from him.

"Well, I've heard it said that in Alaska, if you don't have a nickname by the second month you're here, you really don't belong here."

"I guess I better get me a nickname, pretty soon, then, if that's the case."

Tom felt easy with the tall stranger who had helped himself to his property and his firewood, but he was still trying to figure out why this guy, who "blew into town" just yesterday would end up at his place.

"I suppose you're wondering why I am out here on your land."

"As a matter of fact, that question keeps popping up in my mind. With all the miles and miles of land out here, why are you on my land?"

"Well," Karl drawled out his "well" in a sing-song tone and said, "I asked in town if there might be any-one in town who was in the process of building a cabin and needed some expert help, another pair of hands and a lot of muscle. You got a lot of votes for a candidate in that predicament."

"And you want to help me out."

"Well" — the same sing-song "well" — "as a matter of fact, yes. I've done quite a few things in my day, and I love building cabins more than anything else I've done, except maybe for making furniture from trees I cut down."

"Let's have some coffee, Karl — I mean Moose."

"Wouldn't mind that one bit. Did you make that meat cache?"

"Yes."

"You did a good piece of work. I hope the little person who has a lot of paraphernalia stashed in the cache doesn't mind my stretching out up there for my nap."

"Nah, she wouldn't mind. She's Queen of the Universe when she's up there. It has turned out to be a kind of playpen for her. We don't have to wonder where she is all the time." Tom put the iron plate on the leveled stones and set the coffee pot on it to perk.

Moose poked the wood and maneuvered the hottest part under the makeshift stove.

"So, how long have you been up here?" Tom asked.

"You mean up here on your land, or up here in Alaska?"

" Alaska is the more important of the two."

"Well, let's start with your land. I have been here about five or six hours. Just the right amount of sleep time. For the second part of the question, I have been up here in Alaska for a little over fifteen years. I have been moving around, seeing as much of this place as I can. I must confess this Kenai Peninsula is the most beautiful, so far as scenery goes."

They talked on about Moose's adventures. Tom felt good about talking to him about the prospects in Alaska's future for himself.

Tom handed Moose a cup of steaming coffee, and poured his own. They sat and talked for another fifteen minutes, then planned a whole day's worth of work for Moose. So much for peace and quiet and sorting out my own thoughts, Tom mused.

The two men worked steadily at their agreed upon tasks, and Tom noticed the ease and grace with which the huge man did everything. They got more done in ten hours than he and his makeshift crews could do in four days.

Moose became a familiar sight on the homestead, and the cabin seemed to turn into a finished product overnight. He made a beautiful trestle table and six matching benches that fit perfectly under the table. The next projects were beds, then chests for storage and shelves everywhere that Tide pointed.

The family sort of adopted big Moose as one of their own and enjoyed his company as well as his skills. Tide discovered he was very well read, and they spent many hours discussing favorite books and reciting lines from poems and plays.

Moose also spent time with an older man, called Mr. Watson, who lived by himself in a cabin not far from the Bowman homestead. Mr. Watson was about eighty years old, and had lived in Homer for over twenty-five years. Moose fixed up a small shed on the property for himself, in order to care for Mr. Watson, who was recovering from a severe cut on his leg, under his knee cap. With his scythe, he had severed all the tendons that operated the knee cap, when he tripped going up a steep hill to cut some grass.

Mr. Watson was a very interesting man with a colorful past. Moose told the Bowmans that the man was from an island off Australia and that he had been in almost every country in the world. He had shelves full of excellent books in his immaculate cabin. His gardens and yard were beautiful. Through Moose, the

Bowmans had a small lending library available to them, and Mr. Watson had hot dinners provided by Tide. Tom and Tide enjoyed visiting with this mysterious, cultured man who preferred to live alone in Homer, Alaska.

Alice was Moose's pet. He would hoist her up in the air, put her on his massive shoulders, and walk around, continuing with the task he was working on, always regaling her with wonderful stories and yarns he recalled or made up. Alice looked like some miniature queen on the shoulder of her giant, blonde, curly-haired slave.

The Haynes and McKinley families invited the Bowmans to go across the bay with them. The Bowmans were excited to be asked again to go on their friends' boat. Alice asked if Moose could come, too. She was anxious to get him to teach her some more notes and fingering on the little recorder he had made for her.

Phil McKinley said, "No problem. Plenty of room. Even for a passenger as big as Alice's friend, Moose."

They left early one morning when the tides were just right for clamming. The McKinleys had a friend who lived over in Peterson Bay, and he often asked them over for kayaking and clamming. The trip across was idyllic, with just enough sunshine to keep off the chill of the breezes blowing across the crystal blue water. They motored around Gull Island, which delighted the four little girls.

Diane and Susan already knew the names, and some of the habits, of the shorebirds clustered together on the little peaked islands. Sybil's favorites were the puffins, but Alice's were the graceful cormorants. Moose said cormorants were his favorites, too.

"These guys are lucky to be living here," he said. "They can eat all the fish they can catch, but their Chinese cousins have to wear bands around their necks and strings on one of their legs."

"Why?" asked three voices, almost in unison.

"Because," continued Moose, "they are fisher birds who do all the work for their Chinese masters. The masters throw the birds overboard, but hold onto the string so they can pull the bird back up after he has caught a big fish."

"Then what happens?" It was Sybil asking, big

eyed as ever.

"Well then," — the two syllable "well" as always — Moose said, "The Chinese lucky enough to own one of these birds, takes the fish from his beak and replaces it with a small chunk of fish."

"How come he only gets a small chunk of fish?" It was Sybil, again, the little detective, who was always searching out whys and wherefores.

"The fish can only eat a little tiny piece, because he has that tight band around his neck to prevent him from eating the big fish he catches."

"It doesn't seem fair," Sybil offered, but she was then quickly distracted by the sighting of her favorite sea mammal. A sea otter and her baby were coming close to the boat. Another joined the first, and they peered at the boaters, just as the people were eying them.

The boat and excited passengers arrived at the

beach and were welcomed by a young man who looked as if he had stepped off the pages of *Robinson Crusoe*. He had no shirt on and his ragged jeans were cut off at the knees. He grabbed the bow line that Charlie threw him and pulled the boat and all the passengers up onto the beach. He tied the line to a ring that was in a big block of cement. Two kayaks were turned upside down beside the block.

"Let's have some lunch!" he shouted, in welcome to the boaters. They all piled out of the boat, introduced themselves to him, and the women began laying out picnic "fixings" on the beach.

The families clammed after the tide went out and filled gunny sacks with the bountiful harvest. They found some blueberry patches and filled more containers with the delicious dark blueberries. They were astounded by the different varieties of plants and sea animals as they explored the "other side of the bay," as this spot is called in Homer.

Although the families hated to have to take their leave from this beautiful bay, it was soon time to go home. The children protested, but they were largely ignored, as the adults packed up the things they had brought. Mothers handed out sweaters and jackets to the children. Their trip back to Homer was uneventful. Most of the children fell asleep in their parents' arms.

One day, just as mysteriously as he had come, Moose was gone. He left a well-worn leather copy of Voltaire's *Candide* for Tide, with a note inside thanking her for restoring his faith in America's educational system. For Alice, he had made a small doll bed that was just like hers, and a little carved dog that looked like Petey Joe. For Tom, he had carved a wooden box large enough to hold important papers, and a carving of the cabin they had just completed together was in the lid.

Inside was a message.

Thanks for all you've done for me. You, my friend, are one very lucky man to have such a splendid family. I enjoyed your company more than any I have ever known. Perhaps our paths will cross again someday. Moose

Alice climbed slowly and mechanically up the ladder into her cache, after they had received and exclaimed about their farewell gifts from their very special friend, Moose. Tom's eyes watered ever so slightly, and Tide moved away from him and walked down the path to the spring house.

Never had any of the three been so moved by a person as each of them was affected by Moose. He seemed almost a myth that they had all made up — another of their bedtime stories — all jumbled, mysterious and enjoyed as each added a part to the plot.

They each kept their own space for quite a while that morning. Having a special fabric of your life torn away suddenly is always hard. But life goes on, and beautiful memories of people you love stay with you forever.

Chapter Eight
Alice Visits Her School

 A week after Moose left, Tide was out in the field by the house, painting a wooden box to use for wood storage, when a jeep turned into the yard. Gene Haduch jumped out and walked over toward Tide.

"Morning," he called out as he approached. "How's everything out in the boondocks?"

"Just fine," laughed Tide, as she walked over to shake hands with him.

"I am actually here on business," Gene said.

"Oh? I'll go get Tom," Tide answered, as she started toward the cabin.

"No, wait. This business concerns you more than Tom, but I'm sure you make decisions together."

"Well," Tide smiled, "you now have my undivided attention. What might this business be?"

As Tom came out of the cabin and over to where Gene and Tide were standing, Gene, jokingly, said, "I really came to see your wife, Tom, not you."

"Oh, in that case, I guess I can take a break."

"I came to ask Tide if she would be able to teach at the high school as a sort of long-term substitute. It seems our new hire does not want to come to Alaska, after all"

Gene told Tide and Tom the terms of the hire and the temporary status. Tide was delighted with the offer, but turned to Tom and asked what he thought about it

He laughed and said, "I was wondering which one of us had to go down to that school to make sure Alice behaved, so I guess Gene, here, helped me make my decision."

51

Alice was delighted with the news when she was told that Tide would be teaching in the same building where she would be in first grade. She whirled around the room in her joy, and suddenly stopped, turned to Tom and asked, "But, Daddy, who will take care of you?"

Alice had a long entry for her journal that night :
MOMMY WL B N SKL N SO WL I PTE JO N
DADDY WL STA HOM THA WL GT LONLE BKE TU
I DU NOT NO WAT MY TCHR WL LUK LIK
I HAV NU SHUS N DRSES SUSN N DIAN GUT NU
SHUS N DRSES TU PUR SYBL HS TU STA HOM
SYBL GUT NU SHUS N DRSES TU ENY WA

The next morning, Tide and Alice drove the jeep to town to see their classrooms. Alice wore one of her new school dresses made by Grandma 'Lizbeth in Snow Shoe. They went into Alice's classroom first. Alice looked around and was thrilled to see the desks neatly lined up in rows.

She slipped into one of the desks and folded her hands on the desktop. She smiled as she looked around at all the things that she had expected to see: an American flag, a blackboard, two pictures on the wall of some men her mother told her were Washington and Lincoln, who were presidents, like President Truman. There was also an alphabet in big letters across the top of the blackboard.

She was pleased to see that the classroom looked almost exactly like the one in the Snow Shoe school where she had been allowed to visit occasionally.

Alice knew she was going to like being a first grade student in Homer, Alaska.

About the author

Sara Budinger Peterson lives with her husband, Jon, two standard poodles and a calico cat, in Homer, Alaska.

Alice, An Alaska Pioneer is her first published work of fiction. She has a doctorate in school administration and has worked in education for over 30 years as a teacher, principal, college instructor, Head of Early Childhood Education for the State of Alaska and education consultant for the State of California.

She came to Alaska in 1966 and has lived in Juneau, Anchorage, Adak, on the Pribilof Islands and in Homer.

About the Illustrator

Dianne Widom has been a working artist and instructor for the past 25 years. She lived in six different Alaskan communities over a 12-year period.

Alice is the second book she has illustrated. The first was *Go Home, River*, published by Alaska Northwest Books.

She is currently living in Fairplay, Colorado, with her husband, Ivan.

ORDER FORM

Copies of *Alice, An Alaska Pioneer* may be obtained by mail, directly from the publisher: **Saranjon's, P.O. Box 980, Homer, AK 99603-0980. 1-907-235-8230. e-mail: saranjon@alaska.net**

Please send me _____ copies of *Alice, An Alaska Pioneer*. I am enclosing $11.95 per book, plus $3.00 shipping and handling. (Add $1.00 per book for more than one copy to the same address.) Total enclosed: $_____.

Mail to:_____ (name)
_____ (address)
_____ (city, state, zip)
_____ (telephone)

Look for the sequel to *Alice, An Alaska Pioneer* in 1999.

ORDER FORM

Copies of *Alice, An Alaska Pioneer* may be obtained by mail, directly from the publisher: **Saranjon's, P.O. Box 980, Homer, AK 99603-0980. 1-907-235-8230. e-mail: saranjon@alaska.net**

Please send me _____ copies of *Alice, An Alaska Pioneer*. I am enclosing $11.95 per book, plus $3.00 shipping and handling. (Add $1.00 per book for more than one copy to the same address.) Total enclosed: $_____.

Mail to:_____ (name)
_____ (address)
_____ (city, state, zip)
_____ (telephone)

Look for the sequel to *Alice, An Alaska Pioneer* in 1999.